This Book Belongs To:

_____

This is a Brand-New Book, Written and Illustrated
Especially for Polychrome Books

Polychrome Publishing Corporation
4509 North Francisco Avenue
Chicago, IL 60625-3808 (312)478-4455

Ashok By Any Other Name

Designed, produced and
published by Polychrome
Publishing Corporation.

ISBN NO. 1-879965-01-1

Acknowledgements
Polychrome Publishing Corporation wishes to
acknowledge and thank Ashraf Manji, Ken
Pillay, Raj Rajaram, Lela D. Johnson, James
Nye, Sue Tohinaka and Kay Tokunaga for their
assistance.

Ashok By Any Other Name

Written by Sandra S. Yamate
Illustrated by Janice Tohinaka

Ashok did not like his name.
It was an Indian name.

Everyone always mispronounced his name. At school, the other children told him that his name was hard to say. Ashok was the only one whom teachers would ask, "How do you say your name?" It made Ashok feel embarrassed.

Ashok wished that he had a plain American name like everyone else.

"Why did you name me Ashok?" he asked his father.

"Be proud of your name," said Father. "Ashok was the name of a great Indian king."

"An Indian name," sighed Ashok. "What good is the name of an Indian king for an American boy?"

Then Ashok had an idea! Movie stars sometimes changed their names. Why couldn't little boys?

The next day at school, Ashok
announced his new name to his class.
"From now on," he said, "call me Tom.
My new name is Tom."

"Hello, Tom," said the teacher. "Hello,
Tom," said the other boys and girls.

All day long Ashok was "Tom". He wrote "Tom" on his homework. He wrote "Tom" on his spelling test. He wrote it on his English paper, too.

Then it was time for Arithmetic.

"Who would like to work a problem at the blackboard?" asked the teacher.

Ashok/Tom liked arithmetic. He raised his hand.

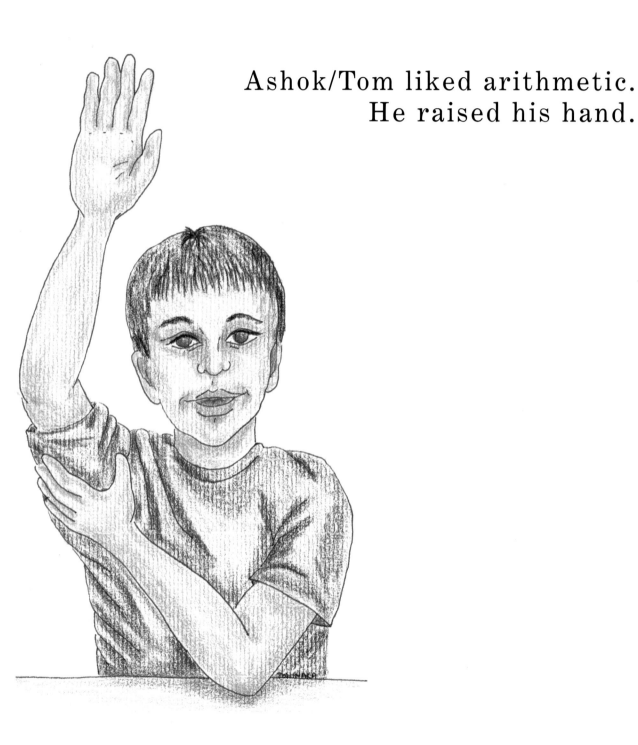

"Tom," said the teacher, "please go to the blackboard."

Ashok/Tom stood up. So did four other boys, all named Tom.

The rest of the class laughed.

"Oh, dear," chuckled the teacher, "we have five boys named Tom in the class."

"Hmmm," said Ashok/Tom sadly, "maybe Tom is not the right name for me."

The next day at school, Ashok announced that he had a new name. "From now on," he said, "call me Walter. My new name is Walter."

"Hello, Walter," said the teacher.

"Hello, Walter," said the other boys and girls.

Ashok/Walter smiled. There were no other Walters in the class.

The morning passed quickly. It was time for English class.

"Walter, would you read the next page aloud?" asked the teacher.

There was no response.

"Walter?" repeated the teacher.

Ashok twisted his neck to look around. Was that silly Walter sleeping? Why didn't he answer the teacher?

Then Ashok noticed that the rest of the class was looking at him.

"Oops," said Ashok, remembering. "I'm the one who's silly. I'm Walter."

Everyone else in the class laughed.

"Hmmm," said Ashok, "maybe Walter is not the right name for me."

The following day, Ashok announced to the class that he had chosen another new name.

"From now on," he said, "call me Francis.

My new name is Francis."

"Hello, Francis," said the teacher.

"Hello, Francis," said the other boys and girls.

Arithmetic and English classes passed uneventfully.

There were no other boys named Francis in the class and Francis would be an easy name to remember.

Ashok/Francis decided that he had finally found the perfect name.

Now it was time for spelling. "Who can spell SURPRISE?" asked the teacher. "Francis?"

"S - U - R..." began Ashok/Francis when he heard an echo. He looked across the room. Horrors! Frances, a girl, was answering, too.

Francis and Frances stopped and looked at each other. The other boys and girls laughed. Frances laughed, too. Ashok did not laugh.

"I knew there were no boys in the class named Francis. I forgot that Frances could be a girl's name," sighed Ashok.

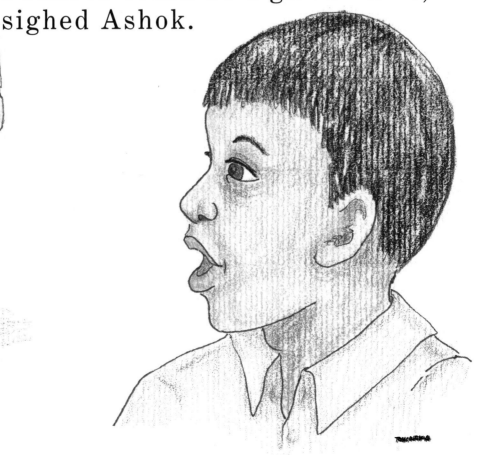

The bell rang. All the children rushed outside for recess.

"Come on, Ashok, or whatever your name is," shouted one of the Toms, tapping him on the shoulder. "You're IT!" He went racing past Ashok.

Ashok shook his head. "I don't feel like playing today."

Ashok sat on the school steps and watched his friends chase each other. At the other end of the playground some girls were skipping rope. Nearby, he saw Mr. Fletcher, the school librarian, reading a book.

"Hello, Mr. Fletcher," said Ashok politely.

"Why are you sitting here all by yourself?" Mr. Fletcher asked him. "Did you hurt yourself?"

Ashok shook his head. "Everyone in class laughed at me." He explained to Mr. Fletcher what had happened.

"Everyone thinks my name is strange," he told him. "Ashok isn't an American name."

Mr. Fletcher looked thoughtful. Then he motioned for Ashok to sit down next to him. "That's probably true," he agreed. "Is that so bad?"

"Yes," said Ashok. "It makes me feel like I don't belong."

"I see," said Mr. Fletcher. "I suppose you've never heard of any government leaders or famous athletes named Ashok?"

Ashok shook his head.

"There's no one named Ashok on any of the television programs you watch, is there?" asked Mr. Fletcher.

"And the hero in the stories you read is never named Ashok...unless he lives in India, not the United States. Is that right?"

Ashok nodded.

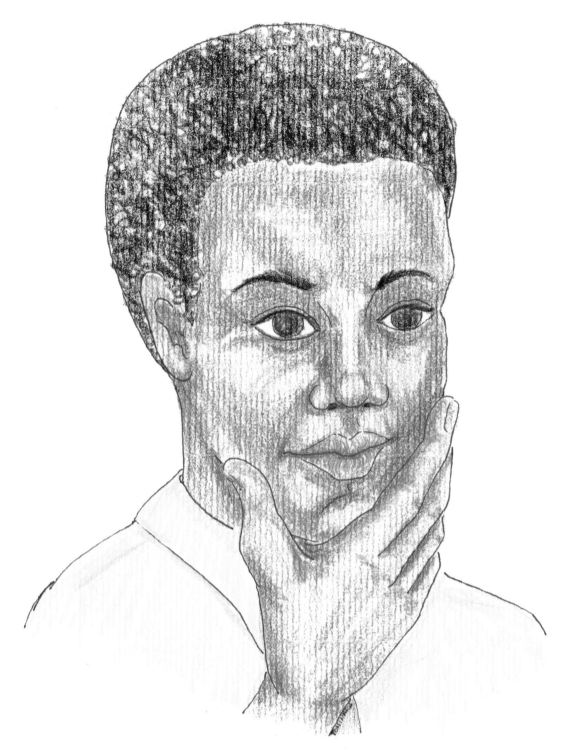

"Yes, that is a problem," agreed Mr. Fletcher. "Still, I think you should feel fortunate to be named Ashok."

Ashok was surprised. "Why?" he asked.

"Well," said Mr. Fletcher, "I can't help but think back to my ever-so-great-grandfather. He had an African name but when he came to this country, he wasn't allowed to keep it. He was given what you might call an American name."

"Didn't he like that?" asked Ashok.

"No, indeed," replied Mr. Fletcher. "You see, he came here as a slave and wasn't given much choice about it. He didn't come here searching for a better life. He had no choice. He was kidnapped from his home, never to see his family and friends again."

"Never again?" asked Ashok in disbelief.

That was sad. Even though he wasn't a baby anymore, Ashok suddenly wished that he was with his parents and they could give him a big hug.

"That's right," said Mr. Fletcher. "He lost his home, his family and his friends. On top of that he wasn't even allowed to keep his own African name."

"Did the African names sound strange? Were they hard to pronounce?" asked Ashok.

"The slave owners might have thought so," replied Mr. Fletcher, "but there was a little more to it than that."

Ashok was silent for a moment while he thought about that.

"I guess the slave owners didn't want the slaves to keep names that would remind them of who they were before they became slaves."

Mr. Fletcher nodded. "Fortunately our country learns from its mistakes and people who come here aren't forced to change their names anymore.

"Your parents came to this country but they were still able to give you a name that could show pride in your family's heritage and culture. My many times great-grandfather would think you are lucky to have your name."

Ashok nodded slowly. "I see what you mean," he said. "Still, it would be nice if some famous American had the same name as me... like the President or a television star...just so people wouldn't think it was so strange a name."

Mr. Fletcher smiled. "Someone has to be first," he said.

Ashok thought about that. "Maybe that will be me." Then he smiled. "I'm going to try. Thank you, Mr. Fletcher."

The bell rang and Ashok hurried back to class. When everyone had returned from recess, he stood up and announced, "From now on call me Ashok. My name is Ashok." Then he added proudly, "Ashok was the name of an Indian king, but now it's also an American name."

"Hello, Ashok," said the teacher.

"Hello, Ashok," said the other boys and girls.

"Hello, everyone," said Ashok.

THE END

King Ashok

King Ashok is more commonly called Aśoka He ruled ancient India for 37 years, from around 268 B.C. to 231 B.C. He was the third ruler in the Mauryan Dynasty that had been established by his grandfather, Candragupta (or Chandragupta) and his father, Bindusara. He is one of the earliest Indian rulers about whom documentary evidence has survived. This is due in large part to the many edicts he issued which have been found inscribed on rocks and sandstone pillars all over India.

Aśoka's reign emphasized righteousness and humanity. He preached and practiced religious tolerance and is credited with enabling Buddhism to grow into a world religion. He banned animal sacrifices and became, in part, responsible for the growth of vegetarianism in India. He undertook to improve communications by making travel easier. He had fruit trees planted alongside roads to provide travelers with food and shade. Wells were dug to provide water and rest houses were built for shelter. He encouraged the development of Indian architecture and art.

Aśoka is revered for his humanitarian principles and the modern version of his name, Ashok, remains popular.

FOUNDED IN 1990, POLYCHROME PUBLISHING CORPORATION IS AN INDEPENDENT PRESS LOCATED IN CHICAGO, ILLINOIS, PRODUCING CHILDREN'S BOOKS FOR A MULTICULTURAL MARKET. POLYCHROME BOOKS INTRODUCE CHARACTERS AND ILLUSTRATE SITUATIONS WITH WHICH CHILDREN OF ALL COLORS CAN READILY IDENTIFY. THEY ARE DESIGNED TO PROMOTE RACIAL, ETHNIC, CULTURAL AND RELIGIOUS TOLERANCE AND UNDERSTANDING. WE LIVE IN A MULTICULTURAL WORLD. WE AT POLYCHROME PUBLISHING CORPORATION BELIEVE THAT OUR CHILDREN NEED A BALANCED MULTICULTURAL EDUCATION IF THEY ARE TO THRIVE IN THAT WORLD. POLYCHROME BOOKS CAN HELP CREATE THAT BALANCE.

POLYCHROME PUBLISHING CORPORATION

STORIES OF COLOR FOR A COLORFUL WORLD

Other Books From Polychrome Publishing Corporation:

Char Siu Bao Boy   ISBN NO. 1-879965-00-3

Written by: Sandra S. Yamate
Illustrated by: Joyce M.W. Jenkin

Hardbound; 32 pages (with illustrations)

Charlie is a Chinese American boy who likes to eat Char Siu Bao (Barbecued Pork Buns) for lunch. His friends find his eating preferences odd and Charlie succumbs to peer pressure. He tries to eat "normal" food only to find he is not happy. Eventually, Charlie finds a way to overcome his classmates' aversion to his ethnic food as they learn to try new foods before they decide that they dislike them.